GRISELDA'S NEW YEAR

BY MARJORIE WEINMAN SHARMAT
PICTURES BY NORMAND CHARTIER

Aladdin Books
Macmillan Publishing Company   New York
Collier Macmillan Publishers   London

For Craig, with love

—M.W.S.

For Molly
and the Morganson's goose

—N.C.

Copyright © 1979 by Marjorie Weinman Sharmat
Copyright © 1979 by Normand Chartier
All rights reserved. No part of this book may be
reproduced or transmitted in any form or by any means,
electronic or mechanical, including photocopying, record-
ing, or by any information storage and retrieval system,
without permission in writing from the Publisher.
Aladdin Books
Macmillan Publishing Company
866 Third Avenue, New York, NY 10022
Collier Macmillan Canada, Inc.
First Aladdin Books edition 1989
Printed in the United States of America

10 9 8 7 6 5 4 3 2 1

Library of Congress Cataloging-in-Publication Data
Sharmat, Marjorie Weinman.
Griselda's new year/by Marjorie Weinman Sharmat; pictures by
Normand Chartier.—1st Aladdin Books ed.
        p.   cm.—(Ready-to-read)
Summary: Griselda Goose attempts to carry out her New Year's
resolutions, but her good deeds backfire.
ISBN 0-689-71341-X
[1. Geese—Fiction. 2. New Year—Fiction.] I. Chartier,
Normand, 1945—   ill. II. Title. III. Series.
[PZ7.S5299Gr   1989]
[E]—dc19   89-31865   CIP   AC

CONTENTS

1. BRAVE GOOSE

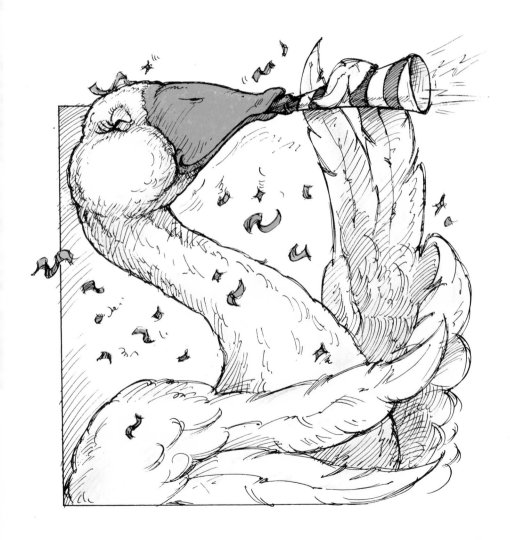

Griselda Goose blew
her Happy New Year horn.
"Happy New Year to me," she said.
"This will be my best year yet."

Griselda picked up her pen and wrote,
THIS YEAR I PROMISE
I WILL BE A GOOD GOOSE.
I WILL BE BRAVE.
I WILL MAKE SOMEONE HAPPY.
"What a fine list," thought Griselda.

GRANDFATHER

8

"I already *am* a good goose.
So that takes care of that!
I have only two things left.
Now, what can I do that's brave?
Grandfather once said
that if I do something
I hate to do,
I will be a brave goose.
I hate to get up
on the left side of my bed
because the floor is hard.
I always get up on the right side
where the soft rug is.
Maybe I will go to bed
and get up on the left side.
That is a very brave thing to do."

Griselda went to bed
and pulled the covers over herself.
Then she pushed back the covers
and got up
on the left side of her bed.
"Ouch!"
Griselda hit her head
against the wall.

She put a bandage on her head.
"Now I'm a brave goose
with a pain on the left side
of my head," she said.

2. THE BORROWED BOOK

Griselda looked at her list.

I WILL MAKE SOMEONE HAPPY.

"Oh, that's easy," said Griselda.

"I will make Brutus Lion happy.

I will return the book

I borrowed from him

three years ago."

Griselda went to her bookcase

and pulled out a book.

"This is it," she said.

She trudged through the snow

to Brutus Lion's house.

"Hi there, Brutus,

and Happy New Year,"

said Griselda.

"Here is the book
I borrowed from you
three years ago."
"Happy New Year to you,
Griselda," said Brutus.
"But you didn't borrow
that book from me.

Nobody has come to my house
for more than three years.
Not even to borrow books."
"Well, I borrowed it
from somebody," said Griselda.

She went to Morgan Goat's house.
"Who is it?" he asked
  as he opened the door
  and tried to push his long hair
  away from his eyes.
"Hi there, Morgan, and
  Happy New Year," said Griselda.
"Here is the book
  I borrowed from you
  three years ago."
"Happy New Year to you,
  whoever you are," said Morgan.
"But you didn't borrow
  that book from me.
  I don't read books.
  All the words look the same.
  Like hair."

Griselda trudged through the snow.
"I *know* I borrowed
  that book from somebody,"
  she said. "I know!
  I borrowed it from Desdemona Dog."
Griselda went to Desdemona's house.
Desdemona was painting it.
"Hi there, Desdemona,
  and Happy New Year," said Griselda.
"Here is the book
  that I positively borrowed
  from you three years ago."
"Happy New Year to you,
  Griselda," said Desdemona.

"But you didn't borrow
that book from me.
I only have books that
tell me how to do things.
Do you have a book
on how to paint a house?"
"No," said Griselda.

Griselda trudged home.
She felt very cold.
She started to shiver.
"I have more goose bumps
than any goose
ever had before," she said.

When Griselda got home,
she put the book away.
"I must have borrowed it
from myself," she said.

3. THE HUG

Griselda looked at her list.
"Oh, dear, I have not made
anyone happy yet.
When I saw Brutus,
he looked lonely.
When I saw Morgan,
he couldn't see *me*
because his hair
was growing over his eyes.
When I saw Desdemona,
she was having trouble
painting her house."
Griselda put on her scarf.
"I must try again," she said.
"And this time I will make
a lot of someones happy."

Griselda went to Brutus Lion's house.

"Hi there and
Happy New Year again,"
said Griselda.

"You're lonely."

"Says who?" said Brutus.

"Me," said Griselda.

"I came to give you
a nice Happy New Year hug.
A hug will take away
your lonely feeling."

"I don't like hugs," said Brutus.

"Everybody likes hugs,"
said Griselda. "See?"
Griselda wrapped her wings
around herself.

"I'm hugging myself,
and I like it," she said.

"Fine," said Brutus.

"Just keep hugging yourself."

"But I want to hug *you*,"
     said Griselda.

She stretched out her wings.
Brutus started to run.
Griselda ran after him.
"You definitely need a hug,"
she said.

Brutus ran from room to room.
"I hate hugs! I hate hugs!"
he shouted.

After a long time,
Brutus stopped running.
"Help!" he called.

"I'm helping," said Griselda.
And she wrapped her wings
around Brutus
and gave him a big hug.
"You're not lonely any more,
are you?" said Griselda.
"No! No! No!" shouted Brutus.
"I knew it," said Griselda.

Griselda went home.
"Nobody who gets hugged
is lonely," she said.

4. THE HAIRCUT

Griselda took
her sharpest pair of scissors
and went to Morgan Goat's house.
"Hi there and
Happy New Year again,"
said Griselda,
and she clicked her scissors.

"You didn't borrow
a pair of scissors from me
three years ago," said Morgan.
"I know it," said Griselda.
"I came to cut your hair."

"Why?" asked Morgan.

"Because it hangs
in your eyes," said Griselda.

"After I cut your hair
you will be able
to see the new year better."

"Is that right?" asked Morgan.

"Positively," said Griselda.

Morgan sat down in a big chair.

Griselda put a cloth
over his shoulders.

"Will this hurt?" asked Morgan.

"No," said Griselda.

She raised her scissors.

"Will this pull?" asked Morgan.

"Never," said Griselda.

"Will I like what I see
  when you're done?" asked Morgan.
"Definitely," said Griselda.
  Morgan closed his eyes.
"Okay, begin," he said.
  Griselda snipped a long piece of hair
  from Morgan's head.
  Then she snipped another.
"How do I look?" asked Morgan.
"More handsome with every snip,"
  said Griselda.
  She kept snipping.
"Can you see the new year yet?"
  she asked.
"Not with my eyes closed,"
  said Morgan.

"You may open your eyes,"
said Griselda. "I'm done."
Griselda took the cloth
from Morgan's shoulders.
Morgan got up
and went to the mirror.
"Blaaaaaaaaa!" he cried.
"You like your haircut!" said Griselda.
"Blaaaaaaaaaaa!" cried Morgan again.
"My hair's all gone.
I want it back."
"You can't have it back,"
said Griselda. "It's all in pieces."

"Paste it back!" bleated Morgan.

"I don't like you
  when you bleat," said Griselda.

"I don't like you
  when you cut," said Morgan.

"Blaaaaaaaaaaaaaaaa."

"Don't cry," said Griselda.

"What can I do?" asked Morgan.

"Sit down," said Griselda.

"And wait for your hair
  to grow back."

  Morgan sat down.

"I'll be back next year
  to see how it's doing,"
  said Griselda.

Griselda went home.
"That's the best haircut
Morgan ever had," she said.

5. DESDEMONA'S DOOR

Griselda got a can of blue paint
and a brush,
and she went to
Desdemona Dog's house.
Desdemona was painting her kitchen.

"Hi there and
  Happy New Year again,"
  said Griselda.
"You didn't borrow blue paint
  from me three years ago,"
  said Desdemona.
"I came to help you paint
  your house," said Griselda.
"I will paint the outside
  of your front door."

"No, thanks," said Desdemona.
"I don't like blue doors."
Desdemona closed the door.
"She will like blue
when she sees it," said Griselda.
She dipped her brush
into the can of paint.
"Brrr. It's cold out here,"
she said. "I wish I had thought of
a warm good deed."
Griselda reached high to paint
the top of the door.
Blue paint dripped down.
"Oh, my," said Griselda.
"It's raining blue blobs,
splotches and trickles.
Maybe I should paint
from side to side."

Griselda moved quickly
and stepped into the can of paint.
"Now I have a blue foot,"
said Griselda.
She put down her brush.

"I feel too sticky and too blue
and too cold to go on.
But I must paint Desdemona's door."
Griselda picked up her brush.
She painted *DESDEMONA'S DOOR*
on Desdemona's door.

Then she went home.

"Now Desdemona will always know
where she lives," said Griselda.

6. A FINE NEW YEAR

"What a fine new year I've started,"
 said Griselda.
"I am a good goose.
 I am a brave goose.
 And I have made
 a lot of someones happy.
 I gave Brutus Lion a hug.
 I helped Morgan Goat
 see the new year.
 I painted Desdemona's door."
 Griselda looked at her blue foot.
 Then she felt
 the bandage on her head
 and the goose bumps all over her.

"But," she said, "there is someone
I have not made happy today.
Me!
I have a blue foot
and a bandage on my head
and goose bumps.
I must do something for myself."
Griselda put on a white stocking.

"Now my blue foot is not
blue any more," she said.
Then Griselda turned her bed
all the way around so that
the head was where the foot had been.

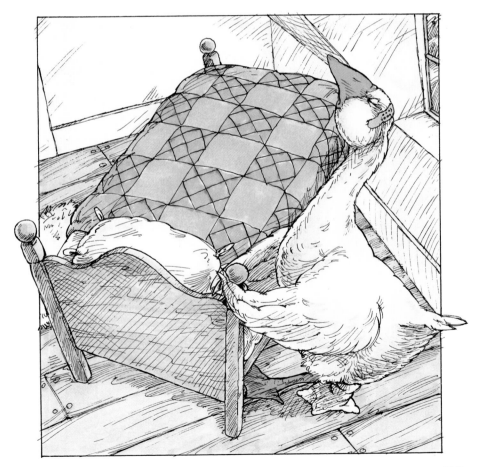

She climbed into bed
and pulled the covers over herself.
Then she pushed back the covers
and got up
on the left side of her bed.
"I did not hit my head,"
said Griselda.
"What a brave, happy feeling."

Griselda got a book
and went back to bed.

She snuggled under the covers.

"A nice and warm

Happy New Year to me," she said.

And she fell asleep.